THE HERMIT'S CHRISTMAS

DAVID de FOREST BURRELL

© 2011 by TGS International, a wholly owned subsidiary of Christian Aid Ministries, Berlin, Ohio.

All rights reserved. No part of this book may be used, reproduced, or stored in any retrieval system, in any form or by any means, electronic or mechanical, without written permission from the publisher except for brief quotations embodied in critical articles and reviews.

ISBN: 978-1-936208-59-3

Cover design and layout: Felicia Kern
Illustrations: Igor Kondratyuk

Printed in the USA
First printing: November, 2011

Published by:
TGS International
P.O. Box 355
Berlin, Ohio 44610 USA
Phone: 330·893·4828
Fax: 330·893·2305
www.tgsinternational.com

TGS000414

THE HERMIT'S CHRISTMAS

INTRODUCTION

This intriguing Christmas tale is set in the Middle Ages, probably toward the end of the Crusades. The Crusades were organized "Christian" military expeditions with the goal of recapturing Palestine from the Muslims and gaining permanent control of it. Most crusaders were Roman Catholics from Western Europe and consisted of kings, nobles, knights, peasants, and townspeople who in the name of Christ ruthlessly butchered Muslims by the thousands. Christ's true way of love, as taught by the hermit in this story, stands out as a gold thread against this dark backdrop of "Christian" hatred and war.

THE HERMIT'S CHRISTMAS

Hermit Theodore lived in a cave all by himself. He hardly ever saw anyone else. Today was Christmas Day and he expected to spend it alone. However, things turned out otherwise.

As the thin, somber hermit stood by the door of his cave, wearing a long robe of goat's hair, he noticed another man far below him between the wooded slopes and the shining waters along the seacoast. The sun reflected brightly on the man's armor when he came out of the forest shadows on a stony shoulder of the mountain far below. Without moving, the hermit watched the man come closer as he followed the path to the hermit's cave. He was climbing slowly because the armor he was wearing was heavy. He had removed his helmet, which he had hanging on his back. Instead of the helmet, he was wearing a white cloth on his head to protect himself from the hot sun. He was using his sword as a walking stick.

Completely worn out, the soldier stumbled over the last stone on the path and threw himself

on the ground beside the hermit, hoarsely calling to him for water. The hermit brought him some water in a gourd, which the Crusader gulped down. After drinking, he wiped his face, still red and sweaty from the hard climb.

"God bless you for that drink, kind Father."[1]

"Do not mention it, my son. It is but a small Christmas gift, since it cost me nothing more than a trip to the spring down there."

The knight started.

"I had forgotten!" the startled knight exclaimed. "True, it is Christ-

---

[1] Although against Jesus' teaching in Matthew 23:9, addressing a person by the religious title *Father* is historically correct.

mas Day! And quite the place to celebrate it!"

"Where you are is not that important, my son, as long as your heart is right for the occasion."

The knight's eyes twinkled for a moment.

"So, you feast on Christmas Day, Father? I would have thought that dried peas and perhaps a little bit of goat's meat would be considered a feast by a hermit."

The hermit smiled.

"That is exactly right, but the truth of the matter is that the food is hardly more important than the place."

Then the knight sighed loudly.

"Ah, but I'm dreaming," he said, "of a great hall in merry England, the boar's head, the foaming alcohol, the songs, and the laughter! I wish I were there, far across that blue sea!"

The hermit smiled again.

"It is true, Sir Knight, that dried goat meat is not the same as a boar's head, and this gourd is not a horn of alcohol. But the fact remains: This is Christmas Day, and you are welcome here."

"And I will stay, kind Father, and accept your invitation! The truth is, I had decided to stay and eat with you if you did not look too long-faced." He glanced up sideways at the hermit's solemn face above him. "My horse has a broken leg and is lying down there on the road along the seacoast. Thanks to God's mercy that my skull wasn't broken when he fell! I saw a path leading through the forest toward this mountain, and since all paths on Mount Athos lead only to hermits' caves, in no time I was headed this way."

The conversation between the hermit Theodore and the knight was interrupted by the sound of feet clambering up the rocky path. A harsh, nasal-toned voice reached them, uttering loud curses upon lands where Christian hospitality could only be found in caves on mountain-tops. Then an unkempt head came into view, followed by a body clothed in rags and patches.

The hermit greeted the newcomer after the fashion of the East: "Peace to you."

The man paused to get his breath, and answered, "You definitely live in heavenly places, holy Father. It would have been a lot nicer of you to put your cave by the road down there."

"Go complain to God who made the cave, you unmannerly rascal!"

the knight interrupted, jumping to his feet. "I can tell by your clothes that you are a beggar. Get going, and beg from richer men."

"Peace, peace!" said the hermit. "All men are beggars at my door—and all are guests—and all are welcome."

"You will be having a full table of guests eating your Christmas feast of dried peas then, Father, because more of your guests are coming over there."

The hermit and the beggar looked down in the direction the knight pointed. Up the steep path labored four more men, one

II

after the other. The three men at the cave's entrance stood waiting their arrival. Finally they came. The knight evaluated each one of them in an undertone as the hermit gave to each his kindly greeting, "Peace to you!"

"The first one is a merchant, and a rich one, judging by his waistline," mumbled the knight, "and the second is a thief. I can tell by his eyes and how close he walks to the merchant. The third—I don't know what he is, but I can see by the expression on his face that he's a brokenhearted man. And number four is a thinker. I can tell by his wide forehead and thin body."

One after another the four newcomers returned the hermit's greeting, each after his manner. He whom the knight had called a rich merchant offered bluntly to pay for a good meal. The thief spoke with smooth heartiness. The brokenhearted didn't say a word. The one with the wide forehead and the uncalloused fingers responded with the courtesy of one who felt at home anywhere.

"I wish you all a fair Christmas Day, good sirs," said the hermit. "I will share all I have with you as a Christmas feast! Come over here

in the shade of this rock and find a place to sit down."

And without further discussion they sat down on the ground, an extraordinary group, while the hermit brought from his cave a large dish of dried meat, a bowl of parched peas, and last of all, an earthen jar of sparkling, cool water. The beggar started to reach for the meat dish when the hermit stopped him.

"If it pleases you," the hermit said gravely, "we will thank the Christ who was born this day."

The beggar pulled his hand back. The fat merchant, who was thinking of reaching for something, stopped. With bowed heads they waited until the brief prayer was said. Then they all set to eating like hungry men.

"Your goat's meat is tough, but gratifying to my empty stomach," said the man with the wide forehead. "But tell me, Father Hermit, you who gave thanks for dried meat and peas, do you consider this humble meal a Christmas feast?"

"I sure do!" returned the hermit vigorously.

"I most certainly do not!" replied the other with a half sneer. "Neither do the people I'm sharing the meal with remind me of Christmas. Tell me, Friend Knight, does this seem at all like Christmas to you?"

"No," said the knight frankly, "only a snow-white, crisp day at home would seem like Christmas."

Sir Beggar? Does this give you any Christmas joy?"

"No," said the beggar with a whine, "if only I were in my own town—ah, there beggar-folk feast at Christmas-tide at the generosity of the rich!"

"Sir Melancholy? Are you experiencing Christmas cheer? No, we do not even need your answer.

"Sir Merchant, what about you? Is this Christmas to your way of

thinking?"

"No," said the merchant between bites, "there's never a real Christmas without a good roasted rooster."

"And you, Sir Shifty Eyes, does this seem like Christmas to you?"

"No," said he, "I see no Christmas joy in this shriveled-up diet."

"Did you hear that, O Father Hermit?" cried the questioner in triumph. "And you say this brings you Christmas joy!"

"It sure does!" answered the hermit quietly. Then, his eyes glancing quickly around the circle, he spoke more boldly, "And furthermore, Sir Philosopher—because that is what I think you are—I am able to tell each of you why you do not experience any Christmas joy from this feast of mine."

"Let us hear it then," said the philosopher invitingly.

"I will start with you first," said the hermit, not paying any attention to the sneer the philosopher was no longer trying to hide. "You are a philosopher, are you not?— I thought so. You have traded faith for human reasoning, and by doing so you have lost your Christ and your Christmas. You are afraid to believe! You refused to believe that God could be manifest in the flesh because you could not explain it. As a result, you have rejected the Christ of Christmas."

The philosopher attempted to interrupt, but the hermit raised his hand to silence him. "No, I did not agree to argue with you, only that I would tell you why you lacked Christmas joy. And that is what I did. You have no faith, that is why. You, who came across the great blue sea in faith that you could find your destination; you, who followed this mountain path in faith that you would find this cave; you, who do not even know yourself, your neighbor, or your world, yet you step out in faith in all these other areas. However, you refuse

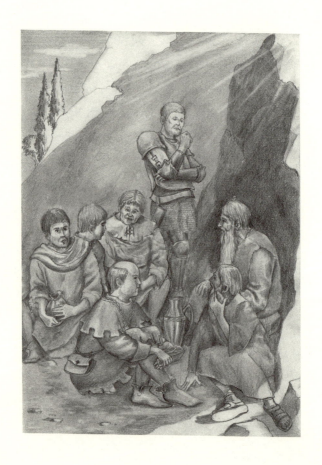

to believe in the mighty finger of God! Not a day passes but that you believe the unexplainable, yet you think you have to explain the Christ child before you can believe on Him! You do not know me; you cannot even explain one of these dried peas. You cannot explain how it grew, or how the sunlight dried it, yet you gladly eat my dried peas! Have I hit the target? 'Whosoever shall not receive the kingdom of God as a little child . . .' "

He paused for a moment. The philosopher's eyes had fallen; his sneer was gone. He had not a word to say. The hermit turned to the thief, who sat next in the circle, and shot his next words at him.

"And you, I know why you have no Christmas joy in this feast! Your problem is that you have stolen money in your bag and a troubled conscience as a result."

The man with the shifty eyes gripped his bag tightly and turned pale under his tan.

"No, Friend Thief," said the hermit more gently, "this is no court of law. There is no judge here but your God. You are afraid to meet the Christ child when you come to judgment. That is why you have no joy this Christmas Day. A clear conscience makes a happy heart. Go back and return what you have stolen!"

The hermit then turned to the merchant. "And you, sir," he said, "I know your kind, if I am not mistaken. I also know the reason why you have no joy in this feast. You have been so busy making money and pleasing yourself that you have forgotten what real joy is. You have lived for yourself. You have filled your treasure chest with gold forcefully taken from your fellowmen. God gave you your talents, but you did not repay Him. You are fat with what you have sucked from God's creation. Your pride is in what you call your own,

and your joy in spending it on yourself. You do not know the Christ child because Christ tells you to give, not to get. You haven't found any joy in this feast because you are thinking only of yourself all the time! The joy of Christ's birthday will come when you forget about yourself!"

When the hermit finished speaking, the merchant grew very red in the face and fingered his billfold uncomfortably. But he did not try to deny the truth.

The hermit's eyes now tried to look into the sad man's face, but the man would not even look up. The hermit addressed him anyway, knowing that he heard.

"And you, Sir Melancholy, it seems to me that I know your sorrow. You consider yourself disappointed. Sorrow and loneliness have become part of your life. Your friends have turned out to not be friends at all. And since you have lost faith in man, you have also lost faith in God. You have forgotten the faith of your childhood. Because of your bitter experiences, you have cursed God."

The sad man lifted his bearded face and gazed at the hermit, his embittered, hungry soul in his eyes. The hermit's tone softened.

"Oh, you poor soul!" he said. "You

have done the very opposite of what you should have done. Instead of false friends you could have a divine Friend. Your house seems empty, yet your Friend prepares a mansion for you filled with friends. You have only looked at the things that are seen, but look up! Look at the things that are not seen, the eternal things of God! Then you will have joy in your Lord's birthday!"

The hermit quit speaking. Suddenly the sad man bowed his head on his arms and started shaking with sobs. They sat in silence until he raised his head and said brokenly, trying to smile, "You have worked a miracle,

Father! This is the first time I have cried in many years."

"I guessed as much," the hermit said, "and tears are often the forerunners of a new joy."

The Crusader was next. With the beggar's help, he had untied the thongs of his armor and removed his shining coat of mail. In his woolen shirt, worn and marked with rust, he was a picture of stalwart strength, with knotted muscles and heavy shoulders.

"You," began the hermit, "you, Sir Knight, have been to Jerusalem, across these Mediterranean waters, to protect the sepulcher of your Lord

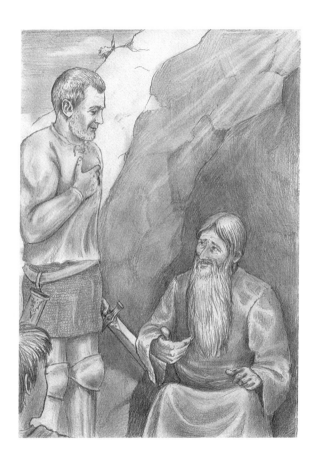

Christ, whose birthday this is. But you do not know your Lord. That is why you feel no joy in Him."

"Not know my Lord!" cried the knight.

"No, you do not know your Lord! I say that for two reasons. First, you have killed your fellowmen, and have waded in their blood, for the sake of your God. You do not know Him because Christ is not served by killing others. You hate the Arab who dishonors your Lord's tomb, but your Lord has commanded you to love the Arab, and you have not heard His voice. Secondly, your Lord Christ wants you to be kind and tender toward all, both man and beast. But you have left your good horse, which has carried you to your Lord's city and this far homeward—you have left him lying down there with a broken leg and have not even put him out of his misery. I repeat, you do not know your Lord. And since you do not know Him, you cannot experience any of His joy on His birthday! You wear the sign of His cross, but if you were really Christ's man, you already would have taken care of your horse!"

At that the knight leaped to his feet. "By this cross," he swore, "you're a very bold man, Sir Hermit!"

His sword was in his hand. The hermit made no move. The others sat watching the shining blade. The knight caught the hermit's eye, hesitated, lowered his sword, and turned and purposefully walked down the path out of sight.

"And you, Sir Beggar," continued the hermit, "you, like the thief, have lived by sucking those around you dry. You've taken from the world and given nothing in return. God made you to work, but you've despised work. Your mind is full of excuses, but not one of them is any good. You are a lazy, selfish,

and unprincipled person. For that reason you do not know Christ. He was a carpenter and His hands were hardened by work. He worked to save men instead of living off of them. And no one has the right to joy on Christmastide who has no respect for himself and no joy in honest work. Stretch out your hand to the plow instead of stretching it out to beg for alms! Let your forehead shine with sweat that comes from working for Christ. Then you'll taste His joy! He has given Himself for you!"

The hermit was finished. He turned to the philosopher with a quiet smile. "Have I not done what I said I could do?" he asked.

The other nodded slowly, then lifted his chin with a challenge. "You certainly have, good host. But I also study men, and I have noticed a problem in your own life."

The hermit's smile faded from his lips. Momentarily he wished to isolate himself. Finally he said in a low voice, "Well, I did not say I was perfect. Neither did I say that I received all the joy I should have from this poor feast. The presence of you all has added more joy to it, yet—I also admit I have known happier feasts."

It was the philosopher's turn to

smile, but he had lost his sneer, and he did not smile.

"You have withdrawn yourself, Sir Hermit," he said gently, "from the world and its snares. You were weak, the evil in the world attracted you, and your conscience troubled you. You, like many others, fled to this wilderness. Is that not true?"

He did not wait for a reply, but leaned forward and pointed at the hermit with a long, slender finger. "And you, too, have lost—not all, but much, of the joy of this feast because you have been a coward! A coward! You were afraid! Though your Lord fought through forty

days and forty nights of temptation; though He agonized for you in the garden; though He showed you how to fight your soul's battles—you ran away to this desert! You had a place to fill, a work to do, men to serve, a Gospel to preach—and you were afraid! And you have only a part of your joy today because you have forgotten that the Christ child whose feast this is was born to help you in your temptations! You have no right to this feast! You should be at your work in the world! Your Christ has a work for you!"

Silence fell upon them all. The hermit seemed to have shrunk into himself. Absently he rolled a parched pea between his shaky fingers. Finally he spoke with a trembling voice.

"I, like the rest of you, am guilty. We are all only needy men. I thought I could keep my soul pure by running away from evil, but"—and his voice grew clearer and stronger—"I was wrong. I will go back! I'll go back to serve my Lord Christ! And you, brothers? What of you all? Will you go back with me to serve our Lord and our brothers?"

He looked around the little circle. No one answered for a moment; then the sorrowful man said, "I will go."

"And I," said the thief.

The others nodded without speaking. All, that is, except the philosopher, who sat with head bowed low, deep in some soul struggle.

"Come on," said the merchant briskly, "if I can break my chain, you can break yours too."

"No, friend," said the philosopher sadly, "it is not chains, but the absence of chains, that I feel. If I could just chain my soul to your Christ—but how can I? How can a man force his soul to accept a mystery his mind rejects?"

Then the sorrowful man answered with a new and more cheerful tone in his voice. "Oh yes, that he can!

That is what I have just done! It's true that my mind cannot see or understand heaven, but I am weary of guesswork. I will believe and hope. And you, with all your knowledge, are not as wise as God. Your mind will not save you; your faith will."

"That is wisdom," said the hermit slowly. "When we talk to you, you don't ask us to explain everything before you believe it. Christ is speaking to you today on His day. Will you argue with Him? Do not argue, just believe Him!

The philosopher looked up at them again, his forehead now free of wrinkles.

"Why, Father, the world was not built in a day. I'll be honest with you. I cannot believe right now, but I will pray that Christ will help me believe. Is that enough?"

"I'm just a poor fool," spoke the beggar, "and you're a philosopher, but it seems to me that if you're praying to Christ, you already believe."

"And that, again, is wisdom," said the hermit.

So they sat and talked while the shadows moved around the mountain and the sun began to sink over the sea to the west.

"When the sun goes down, we will go into the world," the hermit said.

Toward twilight they heard the footsteps of the soldier returning. He stopped for a moment, surveying the scene. They were on their feet, dressing themselves for the descent.

"What now?" he cried when he could get his breath.

The philosopher spoke for all of them. "We have been going to school, Sir Knight, the same as you have. We learned that this Christmas Day takes us back to the world. Will you come too?"

"So," said the knight, the old twinkle in his eye, "what have you learned, wise one?"

"That the joy of the Christmas feast can be found in dried peas if faith is present at the table."

"And you, Sir—excuse the term—Sir Beggar?"

"That the joy of the Christmas feast is his who hath honest sweat upon his brow."

"And you, Sir Merchant?"

"That the joy of the Christmas feast is not in the food, but in finding joy for others."

"And you, Sir Melancholy?"

"That there can be joy in the Christmas feast, even for the bitter soul, if he looks forward, not backward."

"And you, Sir—excuse the term—Sir Thief?"

"That was a good guess," said the thief. His eyes met the soldier's squarely. "But I have learned that there is no Christmas joy without an honest conscience."

"And you, good host?"

"They have taught me, Sir Knight! There is no fullness of joy for him who shirks the fight. We go back to life together. Will you go with us?"

The knight's face brightened. "I will go, and gladly, without my coat of mail. You have taught me too, Father. The Christ whose birthday we celebrate doesn't rejoice in hatred, but in love and kindness to all. You certainly conduct a meaningful school! You have shown us the meaning of Christmas! Master and scholars, all for the world this Christmas Day! May God give us joy in our travels!"

So, in the cool of evening, they all filed down the path from the hermit's cave to the road that led to the world.

ISBN 9781936208593